·El Toro & Friends·

Tacos Today

MON · (TUES) · WED · THURS · FRI · SAT · SUN

by Raúl the Third

colors by Elaine Bay

 VERSIFY

An Imprint of HarperCollinsPublishers

The gang is getting hungry at
Ricky Ratón's School of Lucha!

Every day
is taco day
for you!

TACOS ARE THE BEST!

Tacos today, tacos tomorrow, tacos on Tuesday . . .

You have a tortilla and whatever kind of filling and salsa you want. Everyone has a favorite.

9

El Toro and his friends empty their pockets and count how much money they have.

"Just a bunch of pennies y moscas!"

¡No me digas!
Don't tell me!

We're never
going to eat!

¡Me rechina el estómago!
My stomach is growling!

¡Tengo hambre también!
I'm hungry too!

We are an amazing
TEAM!
We are luchadores
We can do anything!

Inside the bus, all the passengers dance in their seats. Armor Dillo busts a move and Lizarda steps to the beat!

21

The crowd loves them!

The pasajeros shower them with monedas!

At last they arrive at Taco Square.

25

El Toro and Friends walk to the center of la plaza.

"What you are about to witness has never been seen outside El Coliseo!"

"Today you will see los estudiantes de Ricky Ratón in action!"

Armor Dillo sounds the bell and los luchadores launch into action!

El Toro charges!
Lizarda swings from la fuente!

33

Armor Dillo dribbles Croak!
Jack A. López dodges La Oink
Oink's kicks!

More people come to watch!
Everyone cheers and applauds!

41

The taco sellers surround the team.

Thank you for your amazing performance!

You brought us even more customers!

YourTacos are

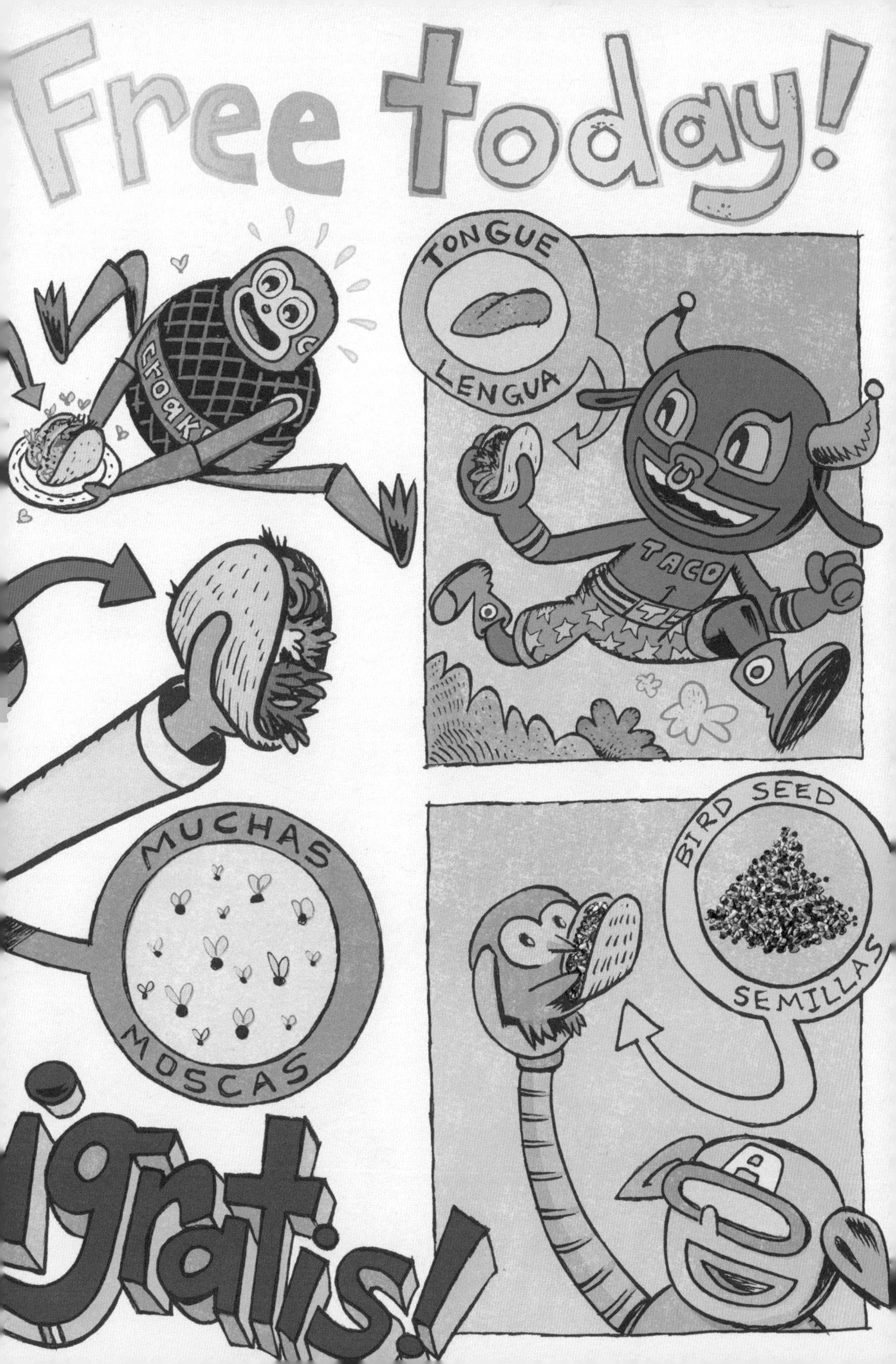
Free today!
Croak
TONGUE
LENGUA
TACO
MUCHAS
MOSCAS
BIRD SEED
SEMILLAS
¡gratis!

To J. Wellington Wimpy: "I'll gladly pay you Tuesday for two Tacos Today." —Raúl the Third

for mi tacooos 🌮 ✦ 🌮 your nachoooos 🍿 —Elaine Bay

Versify® is an imprint of HarperCollins Publishers.

Tacos Today
Copyright © 2023 by Raúl Gonzalez III

ISBN 978-0-35-853937-7

The artist used ink on smooth plate Bristol board with Adobe Photoshop for color to create the digital illustrations for this book.
Hand lettering by Raúl Gonzalez III
Typography by Whitney Leader-Picone
23 24 25 26 27 RTLO 10 9 8 7 6 5 4 3 2 1

First Edition